THIS BOOK
BELONGS TO:

_____

_____

_____

D0258516
07102185

For Zeke and Felix, of course. C.S.

For Maxwell. M.H.

First published 2022
by Nosy Crow Ltd
The Crow's Nest, 14 Baden Place
Crosby Row, London SE11YW
www.nosycrow.com

ISBN 978 1 83994 192 4 (HB)
ISBN 978 1 83994 193 1 (PB)

Nosy Crow and associated logos are trademarks
and/or registered trademarks of Nosy Crow Ltd.

Text © Caspar Salmon 2022
Illustrations © Matt Hunt 2022

The right of Caspar Salmon to be identified as the author of this work and of Matt Hunt
to be identified as the illustrator of this work has been asserted.

All rights reserved

This book is sold subject to the condition that it shall not, by way of trade or otherwise,
be lent, hired out or otherwise circulated in any form of binding or cover other than that
in which it is published. No part of this publication may be reproduced, stored in a retrieval
system, or transmitted in any form or by any means (electronic, mechanical, photocopying,
recording or otherwise) without the prior written permission of Nosy Crow Ltd.

A CIP catalogue record for this book is available
from the British Library.

Printed in China

Papers used by Nosy Crow are made from
wood grown in sustainable forests.

1 3 5 7 9 10 8 6 4 2 (HB)
3 5 7 9 10 8 6 4 2 (PB)

HELLO!

Welcome to a fun new counting book.
Are you ready to start counting?

As we go through the book, follow the instructions.
Don't worry if you make a mistake!

Let's start with something nice and easy.
Do you know what an apple looks like? Good!
Simply count how many apples are here.

Correct! **ONE!**

Now for something bigger . . .

How many ELEPHANTS are on this page?

Yes, that's right. Just <u>ONE!</u>
Now, what about this?

How many . . .

SAUSAGES can you see?

BRAVO!

You are really getting the hang of counting to ONE.
But it's going to get more difficult now.

How many . . .

FLIES are there in the soup?

AMAZING!

You certainly can count to ONE.
That's fantastic!

Right. This is a bit more tricky.

There are quite a few things on this page.
Can you pick just ONE of them and count it?

that are ROLLERBLADING.

No counting the other ducks, please!
In this book, you must only ever count to ONE!

Now for something even more difficult.
Can you handle it? CAN YOU?!

On this page, there are lots of worms –
but only ONE of them is in disguise.

Ignore all the other worms, please,
and count that ONE worm!

BRILLIANT!

So, here we have . . . some rhinos,
a few baboons, a number of snakes,
several ants and butterflies,
and ONE giraffe.

Using your counting skills, please count the giraffe.

I hope you didn't count the other animals.
Remember, this book is about counting to ONE!

Hey, what number comes after ONE?

I'm joking! Don't say it!
The answer will only ever be ONE!
Like this picture of just ONE cake.

Please count it.

Just checking – you **ONLY** counted the cake, right?

Because there was **ONLY ONE** cake.
And in this book you are counting to **ONE.**

I think we should go back to the beginning,
just to be sure:

Here is **ONE** apple for you to count.

What?! Did you think you would learn to count
to big numbers like a HUNDRED?!

WELL, NO!

If you really want to count to a big number,
you could go through the whole book and
count all the things from the beginning
to the end . . .

but that would take you all day!

SO – last question . . .

How many goldfish can you see?

WAIT – NO!
DON'T SAY 'TWO'!

I meant to say, 'How many goldfish
are wearing glasses?'

BUT I MADE A MISTAKE!
AND NOW YOU HAVE
SAID 'TWO'!

Hmmm . . . perhaps you're better
at counting than I thought.
I think you deserve . . .

A PRIZE!

Here it is.

(Maybe you'd like to count it?)